14 Days

W9-BCM-698

WITHDRAWN

LITTLE THORN

Written by Jeanne-Ruth Hammer

Illustrated by June Goldsborough

Reilly & Lee Company

Chicago

WITH AFFECTION
FOR MY YOUNG FRIEND
BILLY GARNETT

The new baby was crying.

"Go out and play, Little Thorn," his mother told him. She turned back to the crying baby.

"Go out and play, Little Thorn," his father said to him, and he turned back to the crying baby.

Without saying one word, the little boy went out.

"Little Thorn!" called his friend, Rain Drop.

"Little Thorn!" called another friend, Crooked Wing.

Little Thorn turned away without answering his friends. He felt very cross and quarrelsome. And his friends laughed and ran off to play without him.

He kicked at a stone and thought angrily: "Such a big fuss about such a little baby!"

It was early morning, and the lavender mist
had already begun to lift to the sun. And the
sun had already begun to warm the yellow earth,
while all the breezes hung quietly on the trees.
The leaves on the trees did not move, and Little
River behind the pueblo laughed so low that even
the pebbles and rocks in the water couldn't hear
her. It was the beginning of another day, but
Little Thorn was bored, bored, bored — and un-
happy.

He looked up to the top of the ladder that
led to his home, and he could see the many rows
of wood. They whispered to him: "Little brother,
little brother, little brother; not you, not you!"

Little Thorn felt a great hurt in his heart. If only somebody would come down those steps and make a fuss about **him**. He picked up a pebble and threw it at a lazy lizard, and the lizard scurried away to another sunpatch. He scratched his head slowly, turning, and looked around at the little green bits of baby grass near a splish-splashing spring.

He looked at the houses. His fancy was caught for a moment by the way the sunlight had begun to play on the shelf in front of the door of his home. A thought flew past him: "Rain Drop's house is over my house, and Crooked Wing's house is over Rain Drop's house! How funny. Each house makes a shelf for the house over it so I can play there with Rain Drop and Crooked Wing. The new baby cannot build a house, but I can!"

Every morning the place brought something new to the boy's inquisitive mind, but this day seemed as uninteresting as the **piki** his mother baked every day — those flat yellow cornmeal cakes that she baked on the hot stones.

The rain had come during the night and made the green grass brighter. The rain had opened the blossoms with dabs of blue and pink and gold, but Little Thorn didn't see the happy colors, or else he just didn't care.

His eyes caught the gleam of Little River wandering down to—Where? He looked around, and you could almost see mischief tugging at the straight black hair at his shoulders. Little Thorn's boredom flew away like an arrow from his new bow. A trip! of course. That would be just the thing to make his parents sit up and take notice. They would see, they would, that Little Thorn was much smarter than that new baby.

At first Little Thorn strolled along, poking a blade of grass at his nose, lazily. But his dark brown eyes were not lazy. Bright lights danced in them! He walked quicker. The blade of grass was in his mouth now, and he began to run. He ran along the brown and green skirt of Little River.

Little Thorn called out to Little River: "I have a new baby brother, Little River, and he is so ugly, Little River!"

Little River giggled at him, and kept on running. Little Thorn ran after her, and called out to her again: "I'm tired, Little River, let's stop and rest for a while!"

But Little River would not stop even for a moment. Little Thorn did not stop either.

Now Little River called: "Come on, Little Thorn! Run faster — come with me to Where!" And Little Thorn ran faster, shouting back: "Where!" laughing breathlessly.

Little River grew fatter; her song became softer. Then, before he could think, Little River had run faster than he. She had run right into the arms of her mother, Big Pond.

"Little River, Oh Little River! Where are you? Come back and play with me. Let's go to Where!" But Little River did not answer, and Big Pond looked on quietly.

Little Thorn sat down and dabbled his brown feet in Big Pond. He was hungry and there was nothing to eat, but he would not go home. He remembered that his new brother was there. He played with the sand, and then he built a house with bright blue stones and green stones and a pile of sand.

All this time Big Pond's coolness caressed him gently. As Big Pond sang to him softly, he fell asleep and big cottonwood tree stood watch over him.

The sky sparkled a wonderful blue and the clear dry air did not whisper a sound. Even the quail flew up from her nest as silently as the brush of a blue fly against a blue flower. Big Pond hummed under her breath; if you listened carefully, you could hear the song she was singing. It was all about Little Thorn and his mother and father. It was about his new brother who was so ugly.

While he slept, Little Thorn dreamed of strange men and of the deadly side-winder rattlesnake. He dreamed of his father and his mother, and he moved restlessly in his deep sleep.

Great Sun thought of going to bed soon, and he spread out a coverlet for himself of pink and pale blue and crimson on silky gold. The breezes awoke and drew smiles on Big Pond's face. They played with Little Thorn's hair until at last Little Thorn opened his eyes.

His dark eyes met the dark eyes of a baby coyote who sat a few feet away from him. The young prairie wolf stared at Little Thorn, and the boy stared back at him without moving. Little Thorn drew a deep, silent breath and sat up slowly. Coyote shoved back, startled. Little Thorn sat quietly and spoke in a low voice:

"Come here, puppy, I will not hurt you. I want to play with you. Please — come to me. I will be friends with you. Do not run away."

The coyote moved closer. Little Thorn

moved closer. And he kept up his soft murmuring
to the animal. Little Thorn put out his hand,
open palm up, and waited silently. The puppy
wriggled over, inch by inch, and Little Thorn
moved his hand gently over the puppy's head.
Now he held the animal with both hands.

"Where is your mother, puppy?" and Little
Thorn remembered. His own mother!

"I must go back to my mother! I think she
must be very angry with me for going off with
Little River!"

It was exactly then that Little Thorn saw the blood on the coyote's paw. Gently, he took the paw in his hand and saw that it had been cut. Coyote's eyes were filled with pain and fear.

"Quickly, puppy, we will go home to my mother, and if she's not too angry with me, she will mend your poor, hurt paw." After a moment's hesitation: "My mother is very kind," he crooned to the puppy. "I'm sure she will mend it even if she is angry with me."

Little Thorn gathered the small animal up into his arms and started back on the long walk homeward. He knew very well that he should not have gone off with Little River. He wanted to run, but he walked carefully for fear that the jogging would hurt the animal. The coyote pressed his nose into the crook of Little Thorn's arm.

The stars in the heavens were being hung out to light the earth, and the Lady Moon had polished each one until they shone like his mother's eyes when she smiled at him because he had done something good. But Little Thorn was afraid of the shadows that had begun to rise up and follow him, so he talked to his friend to drown out the voice of fear that whispered in his ear.

"Listen, little puppy, I think that now is a good time to give you a proper name. Before we get home and I am scolded until my ears will be red from listening. You came to me near Little River, and your paw is hurt. You have much courage. You will always be my friend. I shall call you Brave River. I do hope you like it.

"Shall I tell you a story, Brave River?" and a whisper of fear crept into his voice again as he looked from side to side. "It's about a Hopi boy who turned into an owl . . .

"One time there lived a woman in our village who had a very bad temper. When her boy cried, she would scold him and beat him. One day, while she was grinding corn, he began to cry, and his mother got very angry and pushed him outside so that she would not hear him.

"There was a large owl sitting on a tree near the house, and when he saw the boy crying, he flew down and picked him up and took him to his nest to play with his baby owls. The nest was high up in a cave on the cliff near my pueblo. The boy played with the baby owls and was very happy.

"Later, when the woman went out to look for her son, she could not find him. She asked all the people in the village if they had seen him, and she cried because she could not find him."

A picture of his own mother crying too, came into Little Thorn's mind, and he was sorry that he had gone off without thinking about her first. Holding the puppy close to himself, he quickened his step.

"The next morning," he continued, "some men from the village went out to gather wood. They passed right near the bottom of the cliff where the owl lived, and they could see the boy standing in the cave, but already he had started to look like an owl. His eyes were turning yellow, and you could see some feathers beginning to grow on his body."

A faint shiver entered Little Thorn's voice as he looked around him for a moment, and then went on with the story:

"A few of the men climbed up to the cave on the cliff. The baby owls crowded together at the back of the cave; the boy, who was slowly turning into an owl himself, stood apart from them.

"The old owl spoke to the men: 'I know why you have come. You can take the boy with you, but when you get back to your village, you

must do as I tell you. You must put him in a room
all by himself with some good food and fresh
water. You must keep the room closed for four
days, and nobody must look at him during that
time. At the end of the four days the boy will be
a Hopi again. But if anyone even looks into the
room, he will become an owl at once and will
come back to live with me.'

"The men took the boy down the cliff and the boy's parents did exactly what the big owl had told them to do. The father stood guard at the door where he could hear the child moving around inside the room.

"By the end of the first day, the mother became very curious and wanted to look inside. But her husband would not let her. Every day she would beg him to let her take just one peek. For three days he said no, and on the fourth morning she was so impatient to see what had happened to her son that she got very angry and shouted, 'It is almost the end of the fourth day. What difference can such a short time make?'

"She pushed the door open, and right in front of her eyes the little boy changed into a great owl which ran across the floor flapping his wings. He flew up, up, through the doorway out of the house, and away.

"Now the father became very angry, and he shouted at his wife, 'It is all your fault! You did not obey the owl and now our son has become an owl too, and the old owl has another son and we have no child!' "

As Little Thorn ended the story, his voice fell to almost a whisper. He looked around once more. Here and there a piñon tree stood — or a twisted juniper — some even taller than his father. In the twilight they looked like dark stone men. Perhaps, thought Little Thorn, they were men of some distant tribe who had been bad long ago, and the gods had punished them by making them stand still in the desert: hot in the light of Great Sun, and cold in the presence of the Lady Moon.

He thought back to the time he had seen three strangers. They had come to his village and he had heard his father call them some odd name. He remembered their hair — they had worn it in long braids. Not like his own father did, and the way Rain Drop's father and Crooked Wing's father wore their hair, straight to the shoulders. The speech of those men! Hardly a word of it could he understand.

They had come with very nice baskets which had pictures woven into them that his people, the Hopis, always painted on their own pottery. These strangers had asked for the pottery that his mother made, but they only wanted pottery with pictures on them that belonged to **their** own people! It was truly hard to understand strangers!

He remembered, too, how his father had kept putting his hand up to his ear. Just like the time Little Thorn had nearly fallen down the side of the house because he had tried to get down to the ground without using the ladder. Crooked Wing's father had kept looking first to Little Thorn's father and then to the stranger, and then back again. Nobody had seemed very happy.

When the strangers had gone, all the fathers had talked together, so quietly that none of the children could hear. Later, his father had told him that these people did not live in one place for a long time like the Hopis did. He had called them "Utes" — that was their name! **The People Who Wander**. It was such a long time ago . . .

Little Thorn walked close to Little River. The way home seemed much longer now than it had that morning, and there were so many things in the dark that he was afraid of, though he would not tell of them even to his dear friend, Brave River. His lips trembled against his will, and he began to talk again, rapidly and very loudly, to Brave River.

"I haven't told you about my brother, have I? He is very new and very ugly. Yesterday was his name day. And what a celebration there was! With my grandmothers and my grandfathers and all my aunts and uncles and cousins. You should have heard the shrieking that came from that one. You might have thought that he was being drowned instead of only washed. And then, when the clean ashes were rubbed over him to dry him! OH! you should have heard! Why, my ears still feel as though they do not belong to me.

"Do you know what they named him? **Red Bear Cub.** Both my grandmothers wanted that name. They almost never want the same thing, but this time they did. Of course, he was given many other names, but he will only be called Red Bear Cub. He **is** very red, you know, so the name cannot be wrong for **him.** But I am glad that I do not have such a foolish name!"

Little Thorn kept talking against his growing fear: "He doesn't say words, Brave River, he only cries sometimes, and he cannot do any of the things that I can. My mother looks at him just like she used to look at me, and it makes me very angry. Perhaps she doesn't even care that I am not at home."

Brave River pressed his nose deeper into the crook of Little Thorn's arm to tell him that they two were friends.

Little Thorn's voice became thick with the tears he tried to hold back. "Well . . . I think that she really does care . . . but I shall talk only to my father. Only to the men. Of course, I shall talk to you, too. You are my best friend. And when I am bigger and go into the **kiva** for my initiation, I shall ask if I can take you with me. I have never heard of a coyote entering the **kiva**, but since you are my special friend, perhaps the men will let you come in.

"But I'll tell you about that tomorrow. About the Katcina dance that brings rain. But not now," and he looked quickly from side to side.

Little Thorn looked down on Brave River, who had just then wriggled his haunches to tell Little Thorn how contented he was. Little Thorn smiled, but his smile had a worried look in it, and he sighed heavily.

It was quite dark now. A strong hand grasped his shoulder! Little Thorn was brought back to his everyday world. His breath seemed to stop in his chest for half a minute. He held Brave River tightly to himself, and as quickly as the terror that caught at his throat, Little Thorn twisted his straight young body down and out from under the firm hold, and ran.

His father's laugh caught him, and again, his father's laugh was like a rope at his feet, causing him to stumble as he turned. He did not show the joy that pounded in his hungry stomach, but forced himself to walk slowly to the broad-shouldered, stocky man and stood before him, his eyes cast down. The hearts of Little Thorn and Brave River seemed to make a song together, so closely did Little Thorn hold the puppy.

Little Thorn's father said nothing to him, and together they walked to their home where Little Thorn could see his mother standing in the doorway. The smell of burned juniper wood still hung about the place, and Little Thorn could see

the remains of the fire that had cooked the evening meal. The man and the boy exchanged greetings with several of their family who had come out to see Little Thorn come home. Then the father and son went up the ladder, pulling it up after themselves when they reached the entrance to their home.

The boy's mother put her hand on his tumbled black hair. As she broke the silence with "Eat now, Little Thorn, you must be hungry," Little Thorn said to her: "Mother, the puppy is hurt. Will you fix it for us? And will you let me keep him, Mother? Please?" He added, in a low voice: "I am sorry . . . and the new baby is not really **very** ugly."

His mother smiled with understanding and the brightness of her eyes told him that she was happy to have him safely home again.

"How did my father know where to find me?" Little Thorn asked.

His mother did not answer, but only smiled wisely and said to him: "While you and your father eat, I shall wash the coyote's paw and see what else can be done for him. He must be hungry, too."

"His name is Brave River, Mother, and he is my best friend. May I keep him?"

"Yes, if you take good care of him, you may keep him, my son. Think now, do you see how unwise it was to go off by yourself, putting yourself needlessly in the way of danger?"

Little Thorn thought — he thought very hard. Strange. He loved his new friend very much. He loved his mother and his father too, though. Could it be . . . ? Why, yes, of course it could!

While she tended Brave River's paw, the mother sang softly so as not to awaken the sleeping Red Bear Cub:

> "Plants of blooming corn,
> And the bud of butterfly flower,
> Two gifts granted as rain
> Is granted all growing things . . .
> Creator-of-all-Life."